This book is dedicated to my own Walki Talki, London Kai;
mommy thanks you for having so much to say . . .

THIS BOOK BELONGS TO:

....

....

....

....

1309 Coffeen Avenue
STE 1200, Sheridan
Wyoming, 82801 USA
+13179780258 | *www.writersapex.com*

By

DeVona-Rae McGuire

Hello my name is Walkina Wilkerson or Walki for short. Some people call me Walki Talki because they say I talk a lot but I don't think so I just have a lot to say.

This is a story about how I became a Hero.

Mmmm

It was a Friday morning on the fifth of May and it was presentation day, or as Ms. Murphy calls it Walki Talki day. I got the whole class just for me, I think it's because my presentations were so great. I got ready for school early I just could not miss breakfast because it is the most important meal of the day you know. I had oatmeal and a banana.

I was at the bus stop early since we had a new bus driver and I didn't want him to make me late. "Hello, Mr. Bus Driver, my name is Walkina Wilkerson, Walki for short, some call me Walki Talki because they say I talk a lot, but I don't think so, I just have a lot to say. The Bus driver said, "move to the back" without introducing himself. He seemed cranky. He must have missed breakfast, and it is the most important meal of the day you know. That's why he is grumpy.

I politely introduce myself. Hello, my name is Walkina Wilkerson. Walki for short, but some call me Walki Talki because they say I talk a lot, but I don't think so, I just have a lot to say. My presentation is about a frog…

I was sharing with the whole class interesting things about frogs, then the next thing I knew the bell rang and it was time to go home. I think it went well. It was time to celebrate with some Root beer soda pop candy mmmm my favorite. So I went to Mrs. Phipps candy store after I got off the bus. The store is right next to my house. Mama always says, "Be aware of your surroundings". I think that means watch street signs and names. I go into the store to get my candy on the 3rd aisle at the top shelf. I can not wait to spend the rest of my birthday money for a job well done on my presentation.

The next thing I know, I saw a man yelling at Mrs. Phipps with a banana in his pocket and asking for all of Mrs. Phipps's money. I don't know why he has a banana in his pocket, maybe he didn't have enough money to buy the rest of his breakfast and that is why he is asking Mrs. Phipps for her money. He just wanted her to help him out. Mrs. Phipps was looking really scared so I thought I have my headphones connected to a phone that I keep in my backpack. I usually use it to listen to music on the bus while going home. I can call for help if needed, and this seems like a time to call 911, so I duck down behind aisle 3, pull out my phone and call 911, besides Ms. Phipps face says this is an emergency!!

Mike and Ike
Mega Mix
Mike and Ike
SOUR
Mike and Ike
SOUR
Mike and Ike
HOT TAMALES
CINNAMON
SOUR PATCH
Nips
RED HOTS
Ski
Swedish Fish
BAR
DOTS
JUJUBES
JUJYFRUITS
HARIBO GOLD-BEARS
Lemonhead
Lemonhead
GOBSTOPPER
BOTTLE CAPS
PUNCH
PUNCH
PUNCH
PUNCH
Good & Plenty
Good & Plenty
Good & Plenty
Good & Plenty
Good & Plenty
Good & Plenty
Good & Plenty

"911, what is your emergency?" the nice lady said and I responded, Hello 911. My name is Walkina Wilkerson, or Walki for short, but some people call me Walki Talki because they say I talk a lot, but I don't think so, I just have a lot to say and she said, "Hello Walki, what's your emergency? I told her I don't know if its an emergency or not, but there's a man in Mrs. Phipps's candy store with a banana in his pocket asking Mrs. Phipps for all her money, I don't think he had enough to pay for the rest of his breakfast and he must be starving by now since its after 3 o'clock.

The operator told me to hide until the police got here, but I remembered I had some left over birthday money to buy soda pop candy. I can give it to the man so he could at least pay for the rest of his breakfast. I can help!!

I went to the man and said, "Excuse me Mister, my name is Walkina Wilkerson, Walki for short, but some call me Walki Talki because they say I talk a lot, but I don't think so, I just have a lot to say. I have some left over birthday money you can have. You can use it to pay for the rest of your breakfast since I know it is the most important meal of the day.

Next thing I knew, the police arrived and the man ran out of Mrs. Phipps's candy store saying, I GIVE UP!! And with his hands high shouted, "I GIVE UP! I GIVE UP! If you could just stop Walki from talking!!

Oh No! With everything that happened with the police and the banana, I forgot my root beer soda pop candy. I gotta go back to the candy store tomorrow when I get off the bus.

Mrs. Phipps laughed and gave me my soda pop candy for a job well done. Now, when I introduce myself, I say my name is Walkina Wilkerson, but everyone calls me Walki Talki the HERO.......

WALKI TALKI the HERO.......

THE END

Coming Soon: